Largo Bay

Supermarket

Giardini's Pizza

Largo Bay Center

Cinema

Movie Theater

Bloomington

City Hall

Largo Bytes

Comic Book Store

Mayor's Historical House

Gato Village

D0937772

Adventure Begins

Wild and Weird

Blackouts. A bank with no cash. And a historical house mysteriously moves.

Mysterious Lights

One night Abby sees a strange blue-green light. She sets off to investigate.

Ghosts!

Abby discovers ghosts creating chaos in the city.
Will the ghosts take over Largo Bay? Not if Abby
and Clara can help it.

CHAPTER 1

The Big Return

Largo Bay was a fun beach city. People came from all over to enjoy the sun and sand. Through the years the city had grown. Weird things were known to happen there. The oddest things usually happened at night.

It was three in the morning. There was nobody on the beach. Well, nobody living ..

First a blue-green light appeared. It shone far out over the ocean. Three ghosts came out of the light. They floated over the water.

These weren't just any ghosts. One was Palmer Goatsick. Another was Libby Tildren. The third was Mayor Maxwell Davis. They had been alive once. As living people, they had built Largo Bay.

The city had grown. Modernized. The sandy beaches were still there. But there were many more homes and tall buildings. Gone were the open spaces. The place was no longer small. It had lost its rustic vibe.

The three ghosts flew over the city.

"Why … why … those buildings are bad!" Palmer cried.

He had been the city's richest man. Palmer was a city founder. The place was named after his grandfather. Largo Goatsick had settled there in 1875.

Palmer had been rich. *Really* rich. He wore the best clothes. The man had been a friend of Karl Benz. Benz had built a car. It had used a gasoline engine. For a long time, Palmer had the only car in town.

The ghost wore his black hair slicked back. He still looked cool, for a dead guy.

"I would never have loaned money for this!" cried Libby.

She also came from money. Her family had owned much of the city. They had built a bank. It was called Tildren National. The bank loaned money. Its money built shops and homes.

Libby was tall. She always wore long dresses. Her blonde hair flowed down her back. She loved it long. Short hair was not for her.

"Where's my house?" the mayor yelled.

They flew over homes and shops. The ghosts had viewed the entire city.

At first they were just curious. Now they were upset. Palmer, Libby, and the mayor had not expected the change. They didn't know their beloved town had grown.

"There's your home!" Libby cried. "It was moved."

"Moved?" yelped the mayor. "Let me see! Who are they to move my house?" His fat face turned red. The man was angry. His thinning hair stuck straight up.

Wetlands were near the beach. That was where the large two-story home had been. The white home stood apart from the city. That was the way the family wanted it.

Now it had moved. It was next to city hall. City hall was in the middle of the action.

"Well," Palmer said. "At least it's still standing. There's nothing left of the place I remember."

"Indeed," sniffed Libby. "This place is terrible. Large buildings. Small houses. Too many people. My family worked hard. They wouldn't want to see our town look like this."

"You're right," the mayor said. "This is a disaster."

"We can't let it stand," Palmer said.

"And we won't," the mayor cried. "We're going to bring it back. Our people will return. We'll make this town shine once again."

With that, the mayor flew away. Libby and Palmer followed.

The three flew into the blue-green light. In a flash, the light was gone. And so were the ghosts of Largo Bay.

-ᗰ-

"Huh? Lightning?" Abby McQuade said out loud. She stared out her window. The light in her room flickered.

She had seen the blue-green flash. Abby hadn't seen the ghosts, though.

Abby returned to her big bed. She wore her favorite pajamas. Pink shorts. White T-shirt. Her long red hair was in a ponytail. Abby squirmed. She wanted to get comfortable.

She read on her tablet. It was a book by Agatha Christie. The book was called *Murder on the Orient Express*. Her English report was due soon. Abby wasn't behind on her reading. She loved to read. In fact, she couldn't put down this book. Abby had many interests. She could read about almost anything.

Her parents were asleep. The master bedroom was down the hall. The house was perfect for the family. Cozy. It was a one-story home. A few years ago, the McQuades had painted it bright yellow. It was nice to be different.

From her bed Abby stared out the window. What about that weird blue-green light? She had expected to see more. But it probably wasn't lightning.

She turned back to her tablet. Her covers felt soft and warm. Then the battery died.

"No!" she cried. "That's lame."

Ugh. She had forgotten to charge it. Who had time for that? She got out of bed again.

Her bedroom was simple. It worked for her. Less distractions. There was her large bed. The closet was full of clothes. She had a desk too. Like most kids, she also had a TV. It could stream shows. On the walls were photos of her friends.

Abby dreamed of being Katniss Everdeen. Recently, she'd taken up archery. Her bow and arrows rested in a corner of the room. A park was nearby. She practiced shooting there.

Now the tablet was plugged in. She climbed back into bed. But she couldn't sleep.

Should she read another book? There was a stack near her bed. It felt good to hold a book in her hands. Flicking a screen was cool. But turning pages felt real. Studying the words. Feeling the paper with her fingers.

She had been enjoying the mystery book. Abby didn't want to read something else. What about a movie? At 3:30 a.m.?

Abby turned off the lights. She had to be up for school. It was just hours away.

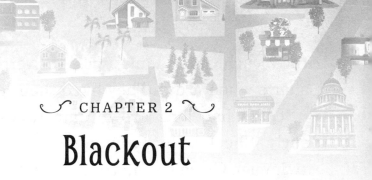

CHAPTER 2

Blackout

School had gotten out 30 minutes before. Abby was sitting in Giardini's Pizza. It was in Largo Bay Center. There were just a few customers. The place was small. There were only four tables to eat at. In the back was a small kitchen.

Abby was getting a snack. She was with Will Chu. Clara Erickson was there too. They had each ordered small pizzas. It would take 10 minutes.

Clara was Abby's best friend. They had known each other since kindergarten. The two girls dressed alike. They mostly wore jeans and T-shirts. It didn't get too hot near the beach. But sometimes the girls wore shorts when it did. They liked their look.

Clara had long brown hair. It was super curly. She was a swimmer—a really good swimmer. Clara was in the sun a lot. Her skin was like honey. Every weekend she had swim meets. Clara liked to win. She hoped to be in the Olympics. Unlike Abby, she lived by the calendar.

Will was into gadgets and computers. He also played guitar. Of course he was in a band. His was called the Psychotic Nebulae. It was a punk rock band.

Will wanted to be a scientist. His grandpa had died of cancer. He hoped to find a cure. Abby knew he would one day. Will was a genius.

The kids were in eighth grade. They went to Largo Bay Middle School. It was close to the shopping center. The mall had restaurants, shops, a supermarket, and a dry cleaner. There was also a game store. It was called Largo Bytes. It sold old video games and comic books.

"The historical center was cool," Will said. "You know what? The mayor's house was moved only a few years ago. It was a big effort."

Last weekend Will had gone to the historical center. It told the city's history. The center showed old pictures and other items. It was next to city hall.

"That's what you did last weekend?" Abby smiled. "That's geeky, Will."

"I think it's cool," Clara said. "Everyone should learn about where they live."

"Thanks." Will smiled.

Abby thought Will *liked* Clara. She knew Clara was crushing on Will. The girl had been since third grade. The two never did anything about it. It made Abby roll her eyes.

"I guess," Abby said. "What's the city's history? What did you find out? That center sounds pretty boring."

"Well …" Will flicked his black hair out of his eyes. He kept it buzzed on the sides. It was long on top.

Will always wore T-shirts. Then he would wear a long-sleeve shirt like a jacket.

"Did you know the city was founded in 1875? There were three main people."

"Wait," Abby said. Then she rested her head on her arm. "*Zzz. Zzz.* I'm getting ready for a long nap."

The lights inside the restaurant suddenly flickered. Then they went out.

"What just happened?" Clara asked.

Abby lifted her head. "I said I wanted to nap," she said. "I wasn't serious."

After a few minutes, a cook came out. A white apron was wrapped around his waist.

"We're very sorry," he said. "We need to close. There's been a power outage in this center."

-♔-

"Wow! You're hungry," Abby's mom said. "Slow down! Don't eat so fast. I made a lot."

Abby sat with her parents. They were eating in the kitchen. Her mom had made pasta. Abby was on her second helping.

Most nights the family ate in the kitchen. Sometimes they ate in the living room. If there was a good show on TV, they would watch and eat. Her dad called it a picnic.

The living room was next to the kitchen. A long hall ran the length of the house. All rooms could be entered through the hallway.

The front door opened into the living room. From that room there were two choices. Enter the kitchen. Or walk down the hall. The hall led to the bedrooms. Abby's was first. Her parents' room was next.

The McQuades didn't live near the beach. The house was on the less fancy side of town. Their neighborhood was closer to Gato Villa and Bloomington. Those cities were a rundown. Houses near the shore cost big bucks.

"I didn't eat a snack after school," Abby said. "We were at Giardini's. Then the power went out. They couldn't cook any food."

"I heard about that," her dad said. "I've had meetings at city hall. I can give them a great deal on solar."

Abby's dad owned his own business. It was called McQuade Solar. He was very excited about it. Mr. McQuade cared about climate change. He wanted the world to be a better place for kids. In his free time, he watched old movies.

Abby's mom was a loan officer. She worked at the bank. Math was her favorite subject. She got to play with numbers. Abby couldn't believe it. Her mom thought math was fun!

"Mrs. Tran had us run a mile in PE," Abby said. "I wasn't expecting that."

The middle school had a big field. The school's blacktop had basketball courts. There were handball courts too. A large track was behind the school. That's where Abby had run her mile.

The school was old. There were three main buildings. One was for math. Another was for science. And the third was for English classrooms. There was also a small library.

"I think there will be more blackouts." Abby's father took a sip of water.

"Really?" Abby's mom said. She got some garlic bread. "Why do you think that?"

"Well," he said. "How old is this city? The population has grown. The energy grid can't keep up. I don't think it's been updated."

"Wait a minute," Abby said. Her mouth was full of pasta. "More blackouts? I'll still be able to charge my phone, right?"

CHAPTER 3

Missing Money

Abby had just closed her eyes. That's when something flashed outside. She blinked. Then she got out of bed.

From her window, Abby couldn't believe what she saw. There were three blue-green figures floating through the sky. They hovered over the city.

"What the heck?" she said out loud.

Abby grabbed her phone. She flicked on the camera. Too late! The figures were gone.

"Darn it!"

She ran out of her room. It didn't take long to reach the front door. Once outside, she felt a sharp wind. It was cold. Who cared? What were those things? She had to know.

Abby couldn't see the figures. She scanned the sky. Where had they gone?

"Abby?" her mom called. She was standing in the doorway. With her white pj's and blanket wrap, she looked ghostly. "Why are you outside?"

"There was something in the sky," Abby said. She walked into the house. "I wanted to take a picture of it."

"It's late," her mom said. "It's one in the morning. Not okay, Abby."

"I was almost asleep," Abby said, smiling sheepishly. She knew it was too late to be awake. Abby could have lied. But she wasn't good at it. Her mom wouldn't believe her.

The girl had never needed much sleep. It bothered her parents that she didn't need more.

"Well," her mom said. She closed the front door. "Just get into bed. Close your eyes. It's good to rest. Your brain needs it."

"Even if I don't feel like it?"

"Yes!"

-⁂-

It was the next morning. The girls had gotten an early start. They had time to walk by Largo Bay Center. Clara was hungry. She needed protein and carbs.

"What's happening?" Clara asked, pointing. She wore a tracksuit. It said L-Aquatic on the back. This was the name of her swim club. Only the best swam for this club. On swim-meet days, club kids had to wear their uniform.

"I don't know," Abby said.

They looked at Largo Bay Center. So many people stood in front of the bank. They seemed to be mad about something.

Many buildings were nearby. This was Largo Bay's business district. The bank was here. So was city hall.

"I wonder what's happening," Abby said excitedly.

"Stop! Not that look," Clara said. "Abby, we need to get to school."

Clara knew Abby too well. Abby was curious about everything. It got her in trouble sometimes. Abby would begin a class assignment. Then she'd get distracted. Eventually she'd finish. Still, the girl seemed to always be racing against the clock.

"We have time." Abby took Clara's hand. They crossed the street. The girls walked past Largo Bay Center.

"Abby ..." Clara eyed her phone. "School starts in 10 minutes. We only have time to get a bite. Don't get sidetracked. Let's be on time for once. There's a meet after school today. I don't want a tardy."

"Two minutes," Abby said. "I promise. Then we'll leave."

"Two minutes," Clara agreed. "With you that means 20."

They walked up to a man. He was sitting

on the hood of his car. The stranger wore a black jacket and sunglasses.

People yelled at the bank. It hadn't opened yet.

"Excuse me," Abby said. "What's going on?"

The man glared at her. "What's going on?" the man yelled. "That bank lost our money. All of it! That's what's going on."

"They lost *all* your money?" Abby couldn't believe it. She looked at her friend. Clara seemed scared.

"Abby," she said. "Let's get to school."

"Everyone's account is empty," the man went on. "The money was there yesterday. Now? The bank says there's a glitch. The cash has disappeared. Every last cent."

The man snapped his fingers.

"Just like that?" Abby asked. "Did it vanish into thin air? I don't get it."

CHAPTER 4

Wacky Jackie

Abby took a seat. It was second period. Time for English.

"Are your tablets ready?" Miss Soto asked. The teacher held a remote.

"Yes," the students said.

Abby thought Miss Soto was nice. The teacher's biggest problem was style. She was tall. Her hair was long and black. Abby figured Miss Soto was around 30. But her clothes were not cool.

"She dresses frumpy," Abby had told Clara. "Like she's *trying* to look like a granny."

Clara had agreed.

"If you've done the reading," Miss Soto said. "You should have no problem."

The class was reading *Animal Farm*. It was by George Orwell. The story was about farm animals. The animals fought their human owners.

Abby had never read anything like it. She loved it. It was different.

Miss Soto pressed a button on the remote. Questions came up on a smart board. The class started to read them.

Then the power went out. Tablet screens lit up the room.

The students cheered and laughed. Abby clapped.

The power never went out. Was the power grid acting up? Abby's father had said it was.

The classroom phone rang. The students' whispers grew into loud chatter.

"Shhh," Miss Soto said.

Many stopped talking.

"What do you think happened?" Piper Espinoza whispered to Abby.

They sat next to each other. Piper was a cute blonde. Abby thought she dressed frumpy too.

"My dad told me the power grid is old," Abby said. "Maybe it needs an upgrade."

"Do you think school will be canceled?" Piper asked. She seemed nervous.

"It should stay open," Abby said. "That'd be cool. Everybody walking into each other. The only light coming from outside. Will the bell work? Probably not. We rely so much on electricity. Today will be like going back in time!"

Piper stared at her. She wasn't happy.

"Okay," Miss Soto said into the phone. Then she hung up. She smiled slightly. "Well, it's your lucky day. There's a blackout. You're all getting a day off."

"That was two weeks ago, Abby," Aunt Jackie said. She ran her hand through her short black hair. Aunt Jackie played with her hair when she was nervous. "And I haven't heard anything since. She's not interested. Or she would have called. She said she was interested. 'Wow! I had a great time.' That's what she said."

Abby was at her aunt's office. Clara couldn't come. She was busy with swimming. Her meet had begun. Sometimes Abby went to cheer her on. Today she took a pass.

Aunt Jackie worked at a legal firm. It was called Clarence & Clarence. Her aunt was a researcher. She loved digging for information. Abby was close to Jackie. She was her mom's sister. Aunt and niece were alike. They were both curious.

Aunt Jackie was bad at dating. Meeting people was easy. Going out was easy. But Jackie had bad luck. Something always went wrong.

"Maybe she's just busy," Abby said.

"For two weeks? Come on, Abby. She's not interested. I just wish she had the guts to tell me. It's silly to ignore my calls. I'm being ghosted." Aunt Jackie was mad now. Her arms were folded.

Abby couldn't help it. She smiled. Aunt Jackie was great. But she thought too much. Her nickname was Wacky Jackie. Abby's parents called her that.

However, her aunt was dependable. She was always there for her family. Aunt Jackie was there for everyone.

Abby and Jackie stood outside her office. There was a small fountain. They were next to it. The office was near the bank. Customers were still outside.

"Did someone really rob the bank?" Abby asked. She looked at the unhappy people. "I called my mom. She couldn't talk about it."

"Someone did," Jackie said. "The question is how."

"What do you mean?"

"Nothing was broken into. There's no sign of a forced entry. No windows broken. No locks smashed."

"Did they steal the money by computer?" That must have been what happened. She knew cybercrime was big. It was easy. Thieves didn't need to be there in person. Money could be moved anywhere. All a crook needed was an internet connection.

"That was checked out." Jackie reached inside her purse. She took out a bag of sliced apples. Abby held out her hand. Jackie gave her a slice. "The system wasn't broken. The money just vanished."

Jackie loved the law. She had friends on the police force. Firefighters knew her. In fact, everyone knew her. She could find out anything.

"Have the security cameras been checked?" Abby took a bite. Apple was her fave fruit. It was so good. She loved the taste.

"Yes," Jackie said. "Cameras were turned off. Somebody didn't want to be seen."

CHAPTER 5

The Floating House

It was a little after 1:00 a.m. Abby moved down the hallway. She wore the warmest jacket she owned. It was super quiet.

She had seen those blue-green flashes. The flashes were strange. The blackouts were freaky. The bank's missing money problem was wack.

Were they connected? Yes! For sure Abby thought so.

The door to the garage was open. Abby pumped her fist happily. She had left it unlocked before she went to sleep. Would her parents notice? They hadn't. Sweet.

Abby quickly went inside the garage. Moonlight shone through the garage's window.

The garage was mostly clean. Earlier, Abby had moved some stuff. The last thing she needed was to bump into them. That would make a lot of noise. Her parents would know something was up. She would get busted.

Abby walked over to the side door. She opened it slowly. It led to the side yard. She walked out. Then she quietly opened the gate.

Abby was on her way.

"Now what?" she said aloud.

She stood at the start of her block. There were city noises, like traffic. But the neighborhood was quiet.

What should she do? Would the blue-green lights come back? She needed them to guide her.

It was so cold.

"If I were a blue-green flash," Abby asked. "Where would I be? Where would I go?"

She headed toward the shopping center. As she walked, she heard the distant ocean. The sound of crashing waves was calming.

Abby turned. She was on the main road. There were no cars. The lights of the center were bright up ahead.

Abby moved closer. She figured she would walk through the strip mall. Would she see anything odd? If not, she'd go home.

"Was it a fluke?" she asked. "The weird lights first. Then the blackout. Finally the missing cash."

Abby continued to walk.

She looked at the lights inside the shops. Hmm, new shoes would be nice. So would a new gaming system. How about a new phone?

Then she looked up. Her jaw dropped.

The mayor's house was flying! It wasn't moving fast. The old house seemed to float. Somehow the historic home was floating! A large pile of dirt clung to the bottom. The home had been ripped from the ground. Clumps of dirt and grass fell over the city.

Abby looked around. Nobody in sight. She

looked back at the flying house. How was this even possible? The house was not small. Will had said moving it was a huge project.

That's when she saw them. The blue-green flashes had come back. Only they weren't flying around. The lights carried the house!

"No way! Those are ghosts!" she cried.

She took out her phone. *Click. Click. Click.* Would the photos turn out?

The home had been next to city hall. Now it was flying away. Abby chased it.

She quickly switched to video. Abby did her best to record what was happening. It was hard!

Was she the only witness?

She never liked running. It didn't take long for her to get tired. Really tired. Abby didn't have much stamina. She even walked in PE. Running was not for her.

But she ran tonight. Where was this house going? She had to know.

The ghosts finally set it down. What? It was in the wetlands. This was where it had been built. At least that's what she thought. Was that what Will had said? She couldn't remember. Will tended to share every detail. People would zone out.

Abby continued to film. It was tough holding the phone. She was so tired.

"Hey!" she screamed. She was almost breathless.

The ghosts floated in front of the house. They looked at this young girl.

"What are you doing?" she called. Her phone was still recording.

The ghosts quickly zoomed away. They headed toward the ocean.

Zap!

The blue-green lights disappeared over the water.

CHAPTER 6

The Investigation

It was Friday. First period would begin soon. Abby had overslept. She had caught up with Clara at school. Students chatted in groups. Others were glued to their phones.

"Abby," Clara said, laughing. "What is this? You can't even see anything!"

Clara was right. Abby's video from the night before was bad. Everything had happened so fast. Abby had been tired and scared. The footage was shaky. The photos were blurry.

"Trust me," Abby said. "Three ghosts moved the mayor's house. They put it by the wetlands."

"How come nobody's talking about it?" Clara asked. "Some kids walk by it on the way to school."

"Oh, you'll hear about it soon. Trust me. The ghosts moved it. I'm going out again tonight. Those ghosts will be back. We need to find out what they want."

"We? Abby—"

"Come on, Clara." The girls locked eyes. "Something weird is happening. We need to find out what it is. Please, spend the night."

"It just sounds crazy."

"I know," Abby said. "I still can't believe what I saw."

"Well, probably not ghosts. You can call me skeptical."

"Look," Abby said. "We'll go out. And if it's nothing, we'll go home. No harm. But if it's something ..."

"That's what I'm afraid of," Clara said, sighing.

"It's our civic duty to do something."

"Civic duty? LOL, Abby! You sound like my mom."

The bell sounded.

"So you'll stay over?" Abby asked. Clara had already started to walk away.

"Sure! But we're only going out for a little bit. I don't want to get in trouble. I've got a swim meet on Sunday. And I'm not missing it. Especially not because you think there are ghosts in Largo Bay."

-ᴀ-

"According to Mayor Bourke," a newscaster said. "The house moved because of a waterspout. It came onshore last night."

"What?" Abby laughed. "There were no storms last night."

Abby and Clara were in her room. They streamed the news. They watched the images on the screen. The before image showed the house near city hall. The after image showed the house at the beach. The new ocean view was great. The wetlands were protected. No other homes were there.

"That's what they are reporting," Clara said. "It's simple science."

"No way is that science," Abby said. "Fake news. Why did the ghosts pick that house?"

"Well," Clara said. "If it was a ghost—not saying it was—ghosts have attachments. Maybe one of the ghosts used to live there?"

"Maybe one of the ghosts is the old mayor," Abby said. She opened her laptop. Then she picked up her phone. "That's it!" she said.

"What?" Clara asked. She sat down on the bed.

Abby typed on her keyboard. A group of images popped up. Some were of the mayor's old house. It originally sat on the wetlands. Another picture showed the town's first mayor. His name was Maxwell Davis. Everyone called him the "old" mayor.

"Him!" Abby pointed at the screen. "That's the old mayor."

"Yeah. So what?" Clara laughed. "He's old."

"He was the first mayor," Abby said.

Abby flipped through the video on her phone. She managed to find a good image. It was one of the ghosts. Mayor Davis!

"Here he is." Abby handed the phone to Clara. She was excited.

Clara stared at it. Then she looked at the computer screen.

"Believe me now?" Abby said, grinning.

"Who are the other two ghosts, then?" Clara asked.

"Let's check." Abby typed.

Clara smiled. She moved closer to the computer.

"So," Abby said. "That's the first mayor. Maybe one of the other ghosts is his wife."

Abby brought up a picture of Mayor Davis's wife. She had a long face. And white hair.

Clara looked through Abby's videos.

"Abby," Clara said with a smirk. "You really stink as a photographer. I can hardly see anything."

"Geez, I was running. It was hard to film." Abby grabbed her phone. She found images of the other two ghosts. They were blurry too. It was better than nothing. "None of these ghosts are her."

"Who could they be?" Clara asked.

"Maxwell Davis was the first mayor," Abby said. "Maybe the others were the first—"

"Founders?" Clara finished.

"Clara Erickson," Abby said. "You are a genius!"

"I try."

"Who founded Largo Bay?" Abby typed on her keyboard. More images appeared.

"Great," Clara said, groaning. "Now we have to look through all these old pictures."

"Don't be neg," Abby said. "One of the ghosts has a name. We just need to find the other two."

"There are ghosts in our town," Clara said. "I almost can't believe it."

Abby found more pictures of Mayor Davis. He was either by himself or with his family. Then she found another image. The mayor stood with two people.

"This one," Abby said.

It was a man. His hair was slicked back. He wore a nice suit.

"That's Palmer Goatsick," Abby said.

"Is that really his last name? Ew."

"The other is Libby Tildren. Says here that Goatsick was a big businessman. The Tildren family basically owned Largo Bay."

"And the bank, right?" Clara asked.

Abby looked at Clara. "Right," she said. "The bank that 'lost' all of its money."

The girls looked at Abby's photo gallery. The images were poor. Still, they looked like the people on the computer screen.

"If that's them," Clara said. "Why did they come back? Why did they take money from the bank? Did they cause the blackouts?"

"Clara, my dear ..." Abby eyed the computer screen. "That's exactly what we're going to find out."

CHAPTER 7

Mall Party

It was late. Abby and Clara were outside. The girls walked toward Largo Bay Center. They wore parkas and beanies. Still, it was freezing cold.

"Why am I risking it?" Clara moaned. "I am going to get in trouble."

Abby ignored her. "Don't think about it," she said.

"How can I not think about it?"

"Think about this." Abby smiled. "You've found ghosts. Real ghosts. People who died!"

"Abby," Clara said, rolling her eyes. "Nobody is happy to find ghosts."

"I am."

The girls stared at the shopping center. It was quiet.

Everything looked okay. The fast food chains, supermarket, and dry cleaner all looked normal. Nothing was happening at Largo Bytes either.

"Okay," Clara said. "Everything's fine. Let's go home. Want to stream *Pretty Little Liars*?"

"Wait," Abby said. "We just got here."

"Maybe the ghosts know we're coming. Did we scare them off?"

"I doubt it."

The two girls stood there. Clara checked her phone.

Abby looked around. That's when she saw something. It moved behind the supermarket.

"OMG, I see something!" Abby grabbed Clara. The girls moved in that direction.

What? They couldn't believe it. There were the ghosts! And they were up to no good. The figures moved quickly. Stucco flew off the building. In seconds the angry ghosts had stripped the place. It used to be off-white. Now the wood frame was exposed.

"They're destroying the market!" Clara cried. "Why are they doing that?"

"We have to stop them. They can't get to the other buildings," Abby said. "Hey!" she yelled at the ghosts. Her voice echoed.

The ghosts looked at the girls.

"It's them," Clara said. "The Largo Bay founders!"

"See?" Abby said. "I told you. Did we scare them? Maybe they'll leave."

But the ghosts didn't stop. They went to Giardini's.

"No! Not our pizza place," Clara said. "Maybe we should call 911."

"Yeah? Why?"

"I don't know," Clara said. "They need to

be stopped. And we're just kids. How about somebody who isn't a kid? Maybe the police can do something."

"*We* can do something," Abby said fiercely. She took out her phone.

"Abby, your pictures suck. They're blurry!"

"I'm not taking pictures," Abby said. "Let's live stream. Everybody will see now."

Abby flicked to Instagram. She clicked the live feature. The stream was about to happen.

The mayor, Libby, and Palmer stopped flying. The ghosts zoomed over to the girls.

Clara grabbed her friend. She was freaking out. It was time to bail.

"Clara!" Abby cried. "Give me a sec. We're almost live."

"So what? There are ghosts here! And they're after us."

Clara dragged Abby to a parked car. They crouched behind it.

Abby clutched her phone. She'd locked it by mistake. The live stream needed to happen. Now! Oh no!

A gust of wind knocked the phone from her hand. It went flying!

"Those ghosts took my phone!" Abby cried.

"Stay down," Clara said quietly. "Maybe they'll leave us alone."

"We will not leave you alone," the mayor said. "Everyone must leave Largo Bay. And then we will stop."

"What?" Abby shot up from behind the car. She stomped her foot.

The ghosts hovered in front of her. They glowed blue-green. The girls were in awe. It was just like the old photos. The ghosts looked exactly the same.

"I mean ..." She took a deep breath. "Why are you here? Maybe we can help."

"Here's how. Go away!" Libby cried.

"But why? Why do you want us gone?" Abby couldn't believe it. She was talking to dead people.

"Because," Palmer yelled. "You don't belong here. Largo Bay is ours!"

"This was a great place," the mayor said. His voice was harsh. "Well, it used to be. Now it looks terrible. It's all your fault!"

"My fault?" Abby was shocked. "What did I do? I'm just a kid."

"We want you out," Libby said.

"We're here for good," Palmer said. "Forever and ever."

"Yes," the mayor said, laughing. "We've changed three things. This town is ours again. Everyone will be forced to leave."

Then the ghosts dashed off into the night.

"Okay, Abby." Clara stood up from behind the car. "I want to go home. For reals."

"Home?" Abby eyed her friend. "We need

to stop those ghosts. Otherwise, Largo Bay won't be home anymore."

Abby looked away. Her eyes searched for a sign of the strange light. But it was gone.

"Right now we have a bigger problem," she said.

"A bigger problem? Ghosts are haunting Largo Bay. They're wrecking it! What bigger problem could we have?"

"I know. I know," Abby said. "But I lost my phone. My parents will be so mad! Priorities!"

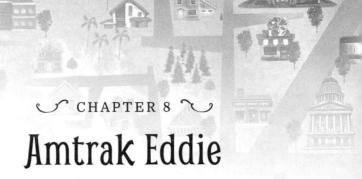

Amtrak Eddie

Abby searched the parking lot. Clara complained. Eventually, the cell phone was found. It was okay! What a relief.

It was almost three in the morning.

The girls walked home. "Abby," Clara said. "I think we should tell your parents."

"Not yet," Abby said.

"Why not?"

"Well, they'll know we were out late. There's no proof at all. You didn't believe me at first."

They continued to walk.

"What are we going to do?"

"Hmm," Abby said. "I want to talk to

Amtrak Eddie. He knows about stuff like this."

-⫶A⫶-

Amtrak Eddie was Abby's favorite uncle. Eddie was her father's brother. He was taller than Dad. His hair was black and bushy. He had a small bald spot on top.

Uncle Eddie was a train engineer. He'd been one for 20 years. His uniform was blue. Blue jacket. Blue button-up shirt. Blue pants.

Eddie traveled up and down the coast. Abby loved his stories. He'd seen so many things. Some were normal. Others not so much.

Eddie was close with Abby's parents. They didn't always believe his stories, though. But Abby did. She thought they were great.

One time Eddie said he stopped a train robbery. Another time he said he saw a ghost train. It had no driver. He called it in. Then it mysteriously disappeared.

Abby and her uncle liked to read. Abby thought that was why they were close. Eddie also gave Abby unusual gifts. Sometimes he'd give her rocks. He'd buy her odd candy.

"Some of the buildings in town were built with flaws." Eddie smiled. "Maybe the ghosts are back to fix them."

"I'm not sure about that," Abby said. "I don't think that's the reason."

The girls sat across from him. They were at a table. It was outside the city's train station. He had bought them hot chocolate. His shift would begin soon.

"You never know." Eddie took a sip of hot chocolate. "A builder could have misread the plans. Maybe the mayor's house was built wrong. Happens all the time. Then the builder quit. Went to his grave full of regret. Now he's back. He wants to make things right."

"The ghosts said something," Clara said. "It was about three things."

"Yeah," Abby said.

"They said that?" Eddie sat up a little in his chair. "Wow! That explains it."

The girls looked at each other. "What?" they asked.

"Ghosts can't come back," Eddie said. "They can't just haunt a place. The ghosts must change three things first. Changing things makes the place theirs."

"They messed up the shopping center. That isn't haunting it?" Abby asked.

"Nope. They can make a mess," Eddie said. "But they have to change three things. Otherwise, the ghosts won't be able to do much. The spirits have to make those things how they used to be. Then they can invite other spirits to the party. What they want to haunt is theirs again."

"Three things," Clara said. She nodded her head.

"They caused the blackout," Abby said.

"The day school was canceled. And the day before that. Remember? We were getting pizza."

"Right," Clara said. "They messed with the bank's computers too."

"Uh-huh. There was only one bank back then. Now it's merged with others." Abby realized what the third thing was. "Whoa! They moved the mayor's house. It's back by the beach. That was the third thing."

"Now they're messing with the shopping center," Clara said.

"It wasn't there back in the day. The ghosts want it gone," Abby said.

"Yeah!" Clara said quickly. "Wrecked shops can't open. Soon none will be left. Businesses will leave Largo Bay."

Abby gasped. "And we'll leave too."

The girls looked at Eddie.

"See?" he said, smiling. "We figured it out."

"Okay," Abby said. "What do we do now?"

"Oh, that's easy." Eddie took another sip of hot chocolate.

"It is?" the girls asked.

"Sure." Eddie leaned in. "Sometimes ghosts forget what they are. They think they're still alive. The trick is to remind them they're dead. Make them see themselves. Like in a mirror," Eddie said. "You can also ask them to leave. Just be nice about it. They'll see they're not supposed to be here. Those ghosts will probably leave."

"Probably?" Abby asked. "They'd better."

"Look, those ghosts may seem evil. They may seem scary. Truth be told? They're not as bad as you think."

"Tell that to our city," Abby said.

CHAPTER 9

All Alone

It was a little after midnight. Abby walked down the street. The night air was still cold. It was so dark. The moon was barely a sliver. There were no cars on the street.

Abby had two things with her. One was her bow and arrow set. It was slung over her shoulder. The other was her tablet.

She brought the tablet for one reason. The ghosts needed to see they were dead. Abby had searched for mirrors in her house. She didn't have big ones.

Why bring her bow and arrows? What would she use them for? She didn't have a clue. An arrow would pass through a ghost. Still, it was good to have.

Clara wasn't with her. The swim meet was early in the morning. Her parents said no to a sleepover. Abby was okay with that. She was brave by herself.

Abby had to stop the spirits.

If she was alone? So be it.

She came to a corner. It was near Largo Bay Center. The ghosts of the mayor, Palmer, and Libby floated in the sky.

The buildings were in bad shape. Giardini's Pizza was almost destroyed. So was Largo Bytes.

The news had warned of more waterspouts. No way! Abby knew what was really going on. And she couldn't believe the lies. This was not right!

"Hey!" she called to them.

The three ghosts looked at her. Then they smiled. The spirits joined hands. A ray of blue-green light glowed through them. The beam of light flew across the sky. It went over the ocean.

More ghosts appeared! The ghosts were dressed in old-fashioned clothes. They headed toward the center.

"We're back!" some said.

More circled around Abby.

"Look at this," the mayor said. "There are more of us. People will leave. The city will be ours!"

"I thought you loved it here," Abby said. "So that's how you show your love? You destroy what had been home? I can't even—"

"You people have destroyed it!" Palmer yelled.

"It's filled with automobiles!" Libby cried. "They smell disgusting."

"Largo Bay was a small town," the mayor said. "A quiet town! And it will be that way again."

"All right," Abby said. "This is cray. You do realize you're ghosts, right?"

The three ghosts stared at her. She held up her tablet. It was filming. Abby wanted the spirits to see themselves. She also wanted a record of it. Would it work?

"See?" Abby looked at her tablet. "You are gho—"

She could not finish the sentence. Her tablet had shut off.

"Darn it!" she cried.

"Enough of this," the mayor said. "It's time for action!"

With that, the ghosts began. They crashed through buildings. Windows broke. Wood splintered. Stucco cracked. If they kept it up, the shops would be ruined.

Abby ran for cover behind a bench.

The mayor, Palmer, and Libby chased her. They were fierce.

Abby ran down the sidewalk. Buildings

crumbled. In the distance, she saw a way out. There was an opening to a furniture store.

Abby jumped through a broken window.

The ghosts chased her. "Out! Out! Out!" they chanted.

Abby ran past beds. She ran past dressers, couches, and tables. Finally she reached the back wall. The ghosts would corner her for sure.

Then she noticed something. A large mirror was nearby. It hung on a big hook. How could she get the ghosts to look into the glass?

"Here goes nothing," she said.

Abby kept moving. She grabbed her bow. Her hand reached for an arrow. She loaded it. Then she pulled it back.

Ready! Aim! Fire!

The arrow flew through the air. It hit the hook! Then it went into the wall.

What? Nothing happened. No way! This was not how it was going to end.

Abby skidded to a stop. She couldn't believe it. That mirror was stuck. Of all the luck.

"What are you shooting at, young lady?" the mayor said. "We're your targets, foolish girl. Look behind you."

The spirits began cackling. They had followed the mayor. Everyone wanted to see the silly girl.

Abby hung her head low. Waves of laughter crashed over her.

The hook suddenly rattled. Then the mirror dropped to the floor.

Crash!

It smashed into pieces. The ghosts couldn't help but look at it.

Yes! They seemed to see themselves in the glass. The ghosts seemed shocked. Did they really look like that? They glowed with a blue-green light.

Suddenly each spirit turned white.

Outside, there was a bright white light. It came from the west, the ocean.

It took seconds. The ghosts headed toward the brightness. They touched it. Then the ghosts became part of it.

Abby put her bow over her shoulder. She followed the trail of spirits. They were leaving the city. The light was drawing them to it.

"I can't believe it," Libby said. She touched the light and was gone.

"That little girl …" Palmer said. As he touched the light, he disappeared.

"We're very sorry," the mayor said. "I guess we forgot. We're not of this place anymore. Our time has passed. We're not supposed to be here."

He touched the light.

Every spirit had become one with the light. It moved over the sea.

Flash!

The light dissolved into the early morning sky. The sea glowed briefly.

Abby turned. She looked at the shopping center. It had returned to normal! The buildings looked fine. Nothing was ruined. Windows weren't broken. Nothing was out of place. It was as if the ghosts had never been there.

Abby looked over at city hall. Mayor Davis's house was where it had been.

"Epic!" Abby said.

Something shiny glowed in the parking lot. She ran to it.

"Really?" she asked, amazed. "Sweet!"

It was her tablet. A streetlight reflected off the glass. Abby saw her image. Mysteriously, the tablet was still recording.

She picked it up. Smile! *Click*. A selfie for the books. Then she walked home.

CHAPTER 10

Grandma McQuade

A few days had passed. Abby and Clara ate lunch. They were with Grandma McQuade. The group sat inside Giardini's.

Grandma lived a few miles away. She always visited Abby and her parents. Clara was like another grandchild. Grandma McQuade loved her almost as much as she loved Abby.

They ordered a large cheese pizza. The girls had convinced Grandma to order soda. Abby and Clara loved Cherry Coke.

Grandma McQuade had thick silver hair. It came down to her shoulders. She was thin but not frail. Her face had lines. But she didn't look old. She wore thick sweaters. Was she always cold?

"Seems like things have been pretty busy here," Grandma McQuade said. "People say this place is quiet. But it has many secrets. And a lot of odd history."

Abby and Clara looked at each other. They both grinned.

Grandma McQuade was very honest. In the 1960s she'd had a top-secret job. She had worked for the government. Nobody in the family knew what she did. And she wasn't saying.

Her first marriage ended quickly. The man was a crook. He was a conman. Grandma helped to put him away. Then she divorced him.

She met Abby's grandpa soon after. He'd passed away eight years ago.

"Let me summarize. First the bank's cash

disappears," Grandma McQuade said. She laughed. "Then it reappears. What a mystery! And what about the old mayor's house? It moved by itself. Crazy!"

"They said it was a waterspout," Abby said. "Everything was caused by a waterspout. And there was a computer glitch at the bank."

"Oh, baloney!" Grandma McQuade snapped. "Do you really think that's what happened? How about the strange light in the sky the other night?"

"It was a lightning storm," Clara said. "That's what they said."

"Yeah. Then another waterspout moved the house back." Grandma McQuade snorted. She looked at the girls. "Don't you believe it!"

The girls had kept quiet. They told nobody about the ghosts. It seemed better that way. Everything had gone back to normal. Abby wanted to tell her grandma the real story. But she didn't. Only Uncle Eddie knew the truth.

Abby changed the subject. "So, how have you been, Grandma?" she asked.

"Me?" Grandma McQuade laughed again. "I'm not six feet under, yet. I consider that a success. Life goals."

Abby and Clara cracked up.

"Grandma McQuade, don't say that!" Clara smiled.

"Why not? It's the truth. I'm even more excited now than when I was a kid. Every day is an adventure. I'm just more distrustful. That's why I don't believe those stories. Here's a real story about lightning. Did I ever tell you two this one? It was about the time it zapped my neighbor."

"No," the girls said.

"Well, I had just started my job with the

government. I lived in an apartment complex. One of my neighbors was old. And really mean. One day he was found dead in his kitchen. The man was holding his telephone. It was right after a lightning storm. Seems the lightning struck a wire outside. He was on the phone at the time. It killed him dead on the spot."

"That's not true," Abby said. "No way."

"Yes way." Grandma McQuade picked up a slice of pizza. "I believe it. There were only landlines back then. None of those funny cell phones. Lightning's a killer. Don't ever take a bath or shower during a storm. It could zap you!"

Abby looked at her grandmother. "I want to be like you when I'm older."

"Me too," Clara said. "You're fun! Feisty too. And you tell the best stories."

The lights in the restaurant flickered. It

was for a split second. Then the flickering stopped.

Nobody seemed to notice. Not Clara, Grandma McQuade, or anyone else.

But Abby did. She squeezed herself. *Don't think too much about it,* she thought. *It couldn't be the ghosts of Largo Bay.* Would they ever come back? That was a good question. She'd be ready for a rematch.

The Amazing Adventures of
Abby McQuade

More Amazing Adventures with Abby

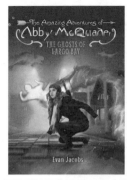

THE GHOSTS OF LARGO BAY
978-1-68021-466-6

VIRUS
978-1-68021-467-3

SCREAM NIGHT
978-1-68021-468-0

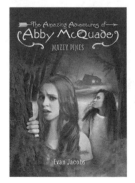

MAZEY PINES
978-1-68021-469-7

BACK TO THE PAST
978-1-68021-470-3